Rescuing Snow White
🔓 Closed Group

Joined ▾   ➤ Share   ✓ Notifications   ⋯

RESCUING SNOW WHITE
is a family-friendly Facebook group
of compassionate and supportive cat lovers.
As of this printing, it is approaching 4000 members.

Over seven million animals end up in shelters each year,
half of which are never adopted. Most pets end up homeless
through no fault of their own. Homeless animals
outnumber homeless people five to one.

Dedicated to:

The loyal Facebook group that supports the efforts
of Rhonda Andersen, in her rescue of abandoned cats.

RESCUING SNOW WHITE

Photos by Rhonda Andersen
Back Cover poem by Idella Edwards

Special thanks to Dr. Craig Smith and his team at
Pet Wellness Center, Ltd. in Marion, Illinois
for their commitment to Snow White's care.

SNOW WHITE

The Princess

Rhonda Andersen

Idella Pearl Edwards

In His hand

is the life of

every creature...

~ *Job 12:10*

My name is Snow White, but I did not
feel like a princess because I was homeless.
A princess sleeps on a soft pillow and eats wonderful food.
She has humans who love her and take care of her.

I didn't have any of those things!

I lived in the crawlspace of an empty house.
I shivered in the cold drafts and dreamed of someday
living inside a nice, warm house. My body had lots of pain, and
my mouth hurt. I knew that my dream was just a dream.
The more I suffered, the angrier I got.
I decided I didn't need anyone's help.

I could take care of myself!

One cold January day, I got caught in a trap
by a human who had been watching me.

I was scared!

I was hungry and in pain, and now I was stuck in a trap.
What was going to happen to me?

The human put me in a "cat condo" inside her warm garage.

She put some food and water in there,
then quietly left for a little while.

I climbed up to the top shelf and crouched in the corner
as far away as I could get.

The next day, the human took me to see her friend, Doc.
He poked me with needles, and his staff shaved off my
grungy, matted fur then gave me a bath. I heard Doc
tell the human that I would need all my teeth pulled out, too!

I just wanted to be left alone!

When we got home, the human allowed me to rest a while and then introduced me to her other cats.

I took a good look at them. They looked happy!
I said, "I don't understand. Why do you trust this human?
She trapped me! She put me in a cage!"

I began to cry.

"Please! Let me go!"

Sam, an elderly lady cat with kind eyes, said,

"Snow White, listen to me! You need to be patient.
The human's name is Rhonda, and she will take good care of you.
You will always have food and warmth and love.
Eventually, the pain will go away.

Believe me. You can trust her!"

Chloe and Finch said, "Yes, we agree. Rhonda is gentle and kind.
Give her a chance. You will love it here."

Rima said, "Rhonda always scratches
under my chin, and it feels sooooo good!"

Neko said, "When I was a baby,
she gave me kisses on my nose!"

Belle decided to tell Snow White a joke to cheer her up.

She said, "Where do kittens go for a field trip?
A 'Mew'seum!"

Silly Belle got the giggles and couldn't stop
laughing at her own joke.

"I know how you feel, Snow White," said Zoey.
"When I first came here, I was frightened, too.
But Rhonda will treat you kindly. You'll see!"

"I just don't know," Snow White replied.
"It all seems too good to be true!"

14

BJ and Neko both spoke at the same time,
"You'll like it here, Snow White. We promise!"

Toby said, "Rhonda loves us, and we love each other, too.
Pepsi and I enjoy our big family!"

"We get to sleep on the beds, and Rhonda doesn't mind
if we lay here all day long."

Diamond asked Snow White,
"Do you want to play hide and seek with us?
My favorite place to hide is in the washing machine,
but don't tell the others!"

"Yeah, it's really fun!" said Belle,
"I like to hide behind Rhonda's laptop, and it makes her laugh."

Diamond added, "Sometimes, I just like to lay in the window and feel the warm sun on my tummy."

I thought a long time about all the things
my new friends had told me. I was starting to feel better.
My fur was clean and soft, and my aches and pains were gone.
I had tasty, nourishing food every day, a warm, cozy bed,
and some of Rhonda's friends gave me
lots of fun toys to play with!

Sometimes, I sit by the window and look outside.
I can see the crawlspace where I used to live,
and I think about my old life. What a difference!

Thanks to Rhonda, I'm living like a true princess, and
it gives me a warm, fuzzy feeling from my head to my tail!

Even my dreams are happy now.
When I lived outside, I had scary dreams.
Now I have a soft prayer blanket that Rhonda's friend made for me,
and I curl up on it and dream sweet dreams.

OK. It was time.
It was time to say "Thank You" to God for my new life.
I asked my friend, Toby, to pray with me.

"Dear God, it's me, Snow White.
Thank You for saving me and for letting me know
what it feels like to love and to be loved.
Amen!"

"Oh give thanks to the Lord,
for He is good..."

~ Psalm 107:1

Rhonda Andersen and Snow White

Rhonda lives in Marion, Illinois with her husband, Jim, and their two children, David and Christine. She holds two degrees from Northern Illinois University and is a Registered Nurse, working in Acute Dialysis.

She and her family are active at Marion First Baptist Church. In her free time, she keeps busy caring for their nine rescued cats and transporting her children to various activities.

Idella Edwards

Rhonda's mother, Idella, was born in Aurora, Illinois, attended Olivet Nazarene University and received a degree from College of DuPage in Glen Ellyn, Illinois. She and her husband, Jack, have five children, twelve grandchildren and have lived in eight different states.

After retiring from the State of Oklahoma in 2005, Idella and her husband moved to Marion, Illinois where they are active members of Aldersgate United Methodist Church. She writes a faith column for The Marion Star Newspaper. She is a member of The Little Egypt Writers' Society and a board member of The Little Egypt Arts Association.

In addition to a poetry book and several Christian devotional books, Idella's previous publications include four children's books, "THE ADVENTURES OF TRUDY THE TREE SWALLOW", "I'M JUST DUCKY", "A VACATION TO REMEMBER" and "HAPPY TO BE ME." Books are available on Amazon.com.

Her favorite pastimes include spoiling grandchildren, working jigsaw puzzles, writing poetry, bird watching and photography.

CPSIA information can be obtained
at www.ICGtesting.com
Printed in the USA
LVRC010536181120
672000LV00001B/6